THE SCULPTOR

THE SCULPTOR TILMAN'S INCREDIBLE AND MYSTICAL JOURNEY IN PURSUIT OF LOVE, DESTINY AND GOD'S GRACE

Klaus Labuttis

ISBN 979-8-9888730-3-7

Foreword

THE SCULPTOR

"Whatever your art is, it will shine and enlighten when you place your skills and virtue in God's presence. Lift yourself up and seize the summit of your visions by guarding against evil and striving for the beauty within God.
Life is generous to those who follow their dreams."

"The Sculptor" is a mesmerizing novel set in medieval Germany. It follows the story of Tilman, a sculptor who embarks on a mystical yet brutal journey to create the most beautiful Madonna.

As Tilman progresses on his journey, he endures suffering, shows unwavering devotion, and seeks redemption, ultimately leading him to artistic and spiritual deliverance. As you follow Tilman's path, you will be immersed in a world where the journey is toward divinity and love.

Witness Tilman's transformative tale as he triumphs over suffering and is illuminated by divine light. His story is a narrative about human beings' search for meaning in life, demonstrating that God may sometimes mislead us, but he never misguides us.

"The Sculptor" is a revelation of how to find one's destiny in the abyss of life. It is an inspiring tale that resonates with the sacred in us, strengthening our faith for spiritual awakening.

With a sculptor's hands, he carved a path to God, whispering, "In each stroke, I find not just form, but the spirit dwelling within. To carve is to commune, and in the grain of wood, I discover the divine tapestry."

Preface

~

Tilman Riemenschneider
Master Sculptor of the Late Middle Ages

As a young man, I was captivated by the rare balance between formal elegance and expressive strength in Master Tilman's sculptures.

I vividly remember seeing his Madonna with Child on a Crescent Moon in Würzburg, Germany. Later, I discovered altarpieces by Tilman in various churches in Southern Germany. His deep-rooted belief and ability to depict the divine in human form touched and changed me.

Even more striking was an anecdote from his life. As a major of Würzburg, an accomplished artist, and an equally successful civic servant, he stepped out of his aesthetic artist-citizen role to become a fighter for freedom and justice.

During the German Peasant Revolt of the early 1500s, his

conscience forced him to confess to his artistic and religious realm. When the forces of the church and aristocracy crushed the revolt, they incarcerated him, ultimately breaking his hands under torture. This was the most severe punishment they could inflict, and no sculpture is known to have been created by him after his release from prison.

Tilman's story speaks of his youth and the suffering that forged him into Being. Without his deep love and belief in the power of God and his Angels, his art could not touch us so profoundly. I will tell you an imaginary story of the famous sculptor, knowing that none of his art would have been possible without his suffering, devotion, and ultimate redemption.

> *The stronger we touch our inner presence, the greater our strength in fulfilling God's work in us becomes. Our firm insistence and fierce devotion do not originate from ourselves but from the grace of God*

Contents

Reaching into the Invisible World

This is love to turn a longing into stillness, become a falcon instead of the dove, nurture the earth so a rose can appear, and give oneself away to find more of somebody else

~

Tilman arrived at dusk at the Virgin Mary's small, crumbling stone altar. An enormous oak tree had grown just beside it. He swept the ground with his hands and used his knapsack as a pillow. Tired from the long, sun-drenched walk, he fell into a deep slumber. His dreams always had the same images: The Virgin Mary would tenderly touch his withered face of old age and hum gently the heavenly little tune his mother used to sing to him, smiling at him.

For Tilman, his dreams were his most precious possessions. Ever since he was a small boy, he deeply loved the Virgin and knew she guided him on his path, giving him strength and confidence. His dreams and inner clarity were almost all he possessed besides the little knapsack containing his thin blanket, a small pot, a knife, and a little wooden horse his father had made for his seventh birthday.

When he awoke, it was still dark, and the sky was a magnificent canvas of opulence with stars so bright that they filled him with joy. As it was his custom in the morning, he knelt and recited a short prayer, thanking God for the beauty of his life. He was content with his simple life and found serenity in it. A tune appeared in his heart, and he hummed it to praise his love for the world and all its creatures. The boy had come a long way since he was born in the small village known as Eichenwald, hidden in a small valley in the Black Forest, owned by Bishop Friedrich in his faraway residence of Überlingen.

Tilman was his given name, and the memories of his mother and father, as well as his younger sister Hildegard, often filled him with sadness and pain. His mother passed away while giving birth to Hildegard when Tilman was three years old. Tilman's father, Gunter, was a kind and gentle man with large hands who loved his children deeply. He tried his best to replace their mother's love with his own care and strong belief in the importance of devotion in life.

Gunter instilled in Tilman and Hildegard the belief that they could achieve anything they desired as long as they had faith in their hearts. He also taught them that fear was the only obstacle that could keep them from their true calling. "The world should not be divided harshly," he would say. "Nothing is better than anything else. Two pigs are not better to have than one, and a bigger hut is not better than a small one. They are different, and their importance is only if God lives in it with you."

Tilman's childhood with Hildegard was happy, filled with

the joy of children's laughter and the comforting presence of their mother, who, even from heaven, blessed their daily lives with her love.

Gunter was a skilled woodcutter who often took his young son into the forest to find the best wood for creating figures of saints or toys. Once, they even searched for the perfect lime wood trunk to make an altar for the modest church of St. Jakob in Eichenwald. Gunter taught Tilman that God lives in all simple things. Gunter's care and focus on his creations inspired Tilman to develop his heavenly beauty. Tilman's spirit was joyful and showed the gift of abundance that God had bestowed on him. He was a flash of color in a grey world, a fountain in the desert, and a cool breeze in the hot sun.

Everybody who knew Tilman saw him steadily change inside to a rose growing to perfection in a splendid garden. With his whole life, he drew closer to God.

So often, his heart seemed to crack at seeing human shapes in the clouds. His sensitivity to all and everybody made people smile. He felt the bark of trees and sensed their quiet, pulsating life. Different stones had distinct temperatures and structures, and the sight of a meadow in full bloom evoked heavenly beauty in him. He longed to be alone, and there was a thirst in his eyes that nothing in the ordinary world could ever quench.

When his father created the altarpiece of Jesus and the Apostles at the Last Supper for their small church, Tilman was spending time with Father Karl, the priest of St Jakob. Father Karl taught Tilman to read and write while Gunter worked on the pews, the crucifix, and other small devotional statues for the church.

The priest, who had dedicated his life to serving God, instilled in Tilman a pure sense of happiness as righteous food that pleases God. Father Karl always told him, "God wants people to find their destiny to harvest their happiness. But this task is difficult because people reap unhappiness, defeat, and desperation more often. And so, the world bleeds wars, hunger, and disease instead of the bliss it longs for".

Tilman learned from his beloved priest that people can consistently achieve their dreams but never realize it. He also learned that this power is available to anyone, even an old man, who can still change his life and bid farewell his unhappy doings.

The priest and Gunter used to sit together in the evening after their daily work was done under the willow tree behind the church. They would talk about the world and their lives. Tilman remembered a particular evening when Father Karl spoke about his father's work and latest masterpiece in a revealing way: "Language is meant to build bridges. Yet, more often, it divides, caught in concepts and abstractions. But art, real art, will always unite. It blows to pieces any division with its purity and mystical assurance. Before true art, every spectator becomes the art himself, forcing him to see his existence".

After some silence, Father Karl continued: "God has nothing hidden from us. We need to open our eyes and hearts to recognize His doings. When we occasionally lose God, we need to look for him where we have held Him. There, He still waits for us to retrieve Him again".

One evening, Father Karl lectured on the divine and the human. He said: "We need to inhibit the space where words do not reach and then speak the language of our heart. With this, we can bridge the gap between the human and the divine by trusting in the unspeakable beauty of the moment and knowing that God is by our side. Man sets himself free by realizing that we contain the seed of God through divine grace. Outward service is the door through which man reaches his truth".

Seeing his father's daily work on the altarpiece, which would become a beacon of splendor attracting people from afar to see it, installed in Tilman the deep wish to create a similar work as a sign of his love and devotion to the Virgin Mary, who visited him at night in his dreams.

But now - these beautiful memories were more trifling reminders of an existence that had perished in the brutality of a power that destroyed everything he had loved and cherished.

Life had completely changed for him. He was alone in this world; all the beautiful experiences of his life in Eichenwald were lost. Tragedy had wiped out the little village and, with it, his father and sister.

Mending a Broken Heart

*When you run away from God, you run right into his arms.
God is always at work. Love him not for any advantage but for
the sake of your Soul. Be empty so he can fill you with divinity.
Examine yourself and turn away from the earthly temptations.*

T ilman had walked for two weeks aimlessly through a landscape of destruction. A deep despair had afflicted his Soul since he witnessed the brutal murder of his family and all the other families in his village. His body became a mere visitor to the necessities of life. His cheerful character was replaced by a deep melancholy. A heavy burden made his youthful frame crooked like an old man. Monsters and demons had invaded his being and were sullying his Soul. An utter darkness manifested itself in his chosen inner prison, and the terrible shadow of death followed him steadily with every step. Tilman awoke every night, bathed in cold sweat since the brutal destruction of his beloved village, Eichenwald. He repeatedly saw the marauding soldiers, ruthless and relentless, approaching the townlet with the sinister intent of destruction.

On the evening, when the terror of death and malice rained down on the village, Tilman had wandered happily in the nearby open fields to welcome spring and its abundance of freshly green shoots. In the blink of an eye, the tranquility of Eichenwald shattered like glass; the quiet, charming hamlet became a scene of chaos and brutality. He heard the cries of the innocent fill the evening, their voices a chorus of terror and despair. Armored in iron and cloaked in malice, the soldiers descended upon the village like an unforgiving tempest. Men, women, and children were herded like lambs to the slaughter, bound by a fate they had no power to change.

The marauders showed no mercy, their brutality a chilling testament to the harsh realities of bloodthirsty men lost to the devil. Tilman could see his father's life being extinguished with a single stroke and his sister's loving spirit snuffed out like a candle in a storm. Tilman had survived by the grace of God, but his world was shattered, and his heart heavy with grief. He lay beside his father and sister for hours after the soldiers had left, unable to stop crying and wailing in the pain that grasped his gentle heart.

~

Tilman spent several nights in the ruined church of Eichenwald. The once beautiful stained glass windows were shattered, and the pews had been reduced to rubble. The moon shone through the broken openings, casting an eerie silver glow and creating strange patterns on the cracked wooden floor. His father's altarpiece, a depiction of Jesus and the Apostles at the Last Supper, still stood untouched. Even the brutal savages who had destroyed the church would not touch such a sacred relic. The wooden figures bore witness to the devotion and artistry that had defined Tilman's father's existence. Tilman felt a deep yearning to create similar objects of spiritual devotion in the silent presence of these holy carvings. He understood that only the quest to create beauty and piety could balance the hatefulness and viciousness that plagued the world. Tilman wanted to find meaning in the chaos and channel his love for humanity into creations of beauty and purity.

He envisioned intricate altarpieces that would speak to the souls of those who beheld them, each carving a vessel of faith and beauty, a prayer in wood. The Virgin Mary, who had caressed his face with her tender hand in his dreams, seemed to speak to him. Her ethereal presence became a source of hope and a beacon of light in his darkness.

Tilman remembered his father telling him about Meister Balthasar, a Master in the Art of Wood and Stone Carving. He was known as the most gifted sculptor in all of Germany, creating figures of spiritual beauty and deep devotion. Meister Balthasar lived in the free Imperial town of Nuremberg in Bavaria, a long journey away from Eichenwald.

As Tilman embarked on the road to Nuremberg, he recalled the words of his father: "To remember that everybody will find their destiny when the clarity within one has chosen a way. Then, everything necessary will be learned on the path, and even experiencing weakness or doubts will only lead to strength and certainty in the face of self-realization. Be wise and see yourself from a distance, aim to improve, and wish to fulfill your task; then you are transforming lead into gold and a simple tree branch into the most beautiful woman."

Remembering his father's words, a stream of deep love rushed from his heart, filled his Being, and made him silent. He understood that to be in the face of God is an endless miracle, an invitation to make one's existence beautiful and meaningful. The pinnacle of his journey would be in creating his masterwork, praising his ultimate spiritual awakening. He put his hand on the wooden cross around his neck that he had made for himself the previous year, and his heart filled with an unspeakable joy and jubilation that he had never experienced. He felt alive in a new way. And this mystery would never let go of him; it stayed like a scent on his Being that no soap could wash away.

He walked on with a firm step, carrying with him the dreams and teachings of his father, the warmth of his sister's memory, and the ethereal presence of the Virgin Mary, who continued to guide him on a path to transcend the ordinary. This path - he now knew - would lead him to the Divine through the Art of Sculpting his visions of beauty and faith.

The Open Road

Reach purity in God; silence your inner grief. Give up your righteousness and accept what he gives you freely in his wisdom. Release your will and made-up assumptions and leave behind your expectations. A powerful prayer needs a quiet mind.

The following day, when the sun was high on the zenith and striking all creatures with its piercing rays, Tilman heard the sound of pipes, drums, and jingles. His heart jumped, and a sweet panic of uproarious joy filled his body. Traveling troubadours were nearby. A tiny village appeared in the short distance, and he found himself confused by the sheer opulence of dancing, singing, fiddling, and jumping when he entered the little hamlet.

The troubadours were a kaleidoscope of talent, each a master of their unique artistry. The village square came alive with a vibrant tapestry of skills and performances. The musicians played melodies that cast a spell on everybody's legs, making them tap and dance. The lutes whispered joyful tunes, the flutes trilled like birdsong in spring, and the tambourines boasted a lighthearted, rhythmic beat.

The music transported the poor village into a dream of giggles and cheerfulness, where the hardships of life were momentarily forgotten. It seemed as though the souls of these withered peasants were beaming carefree for the first time in this world. It was a scene of enchantment, a testament to the power of merriment in the human spirit.

Fools dressed in motley, colorful garments and jesters' caps danced with irreverent pep, their antics a source of beaming laughter. Some wore leaf-like coverings and bright feathered headdresses to accentuate the peculiarity of their cheerful appearance.

They twirled and tumbled, their movements celebrating the absurdities of life. Their laughter was infectious, and the children, with their eyes sparkling like stars, joined the fools in their joyful revelry.

Acrobats defied gravity with breathtaking feats of agility. They leaped and somersaulted through the air, their graceful movements drawing gasps of awe from the onlookers. Jugglers tossed and caught an array of objects in intricate patterns. Balls, hoops, and torches danced in the air, a mesmerizing display of precision. Tightrope walkers traversed slender ropes suspended high above the ground.

The villagers watched in rapt fascination, their daily hardships momentarily forgotten. The spectacle illuminated laughing faces. The gray days of toil and backbreaking work have melted away in the face of such gleefulness. Their tired hands and furrowed brows gave way to giggling for a brief moment, and their hearts sang youthful enthusiasm.

Sometimes, a wellspring of magic and joy can exist, making a pauper king.

Tilman was fascinated and swept away by the scene. For the first time in a long time, a smile appeared on his face. He even heard himself laugh, a sound that frightened him.

Looking at the merry villagers, he sincerely thought about his life and destiny. His inner voice told him, "Never give up my destiny. I remember my childhood dreams, forming animals out of clay and seeing human faces in the clouds and trees. My fate has come in miraculous ways, often as an idea or a vision. I must grasp it with all my might and cling to it like a life savior. Only this certainty will finally free me. I cannot allow my life to bury my dream."

Watching the dancing peasants, he realized they had once seen the light in their youth. They saw the star rising, wrapping them in the warm sunlight of hope and aspiration. But then came the mind, the reason, the world's burden. The heart lost its strength, the idea of failure appeared, weariness and disillusionment followed. Blindness closed their eyes, and responsibility burdened their shoulders. And now all was gone, and only sometimes traces appeared in moments like this when the troubadours bring out forgotten dreams.

After these heavy thoughts, Tilman felt that all this did not belong to him. The jolliness of other people's lives did not fit him anymore. He wandered off, the merry sound slowly fading away, giving space to nature's intense quietness, which responded sincerely with his Being.

~

The day was ending, and the enchanting evening chorus of summer made the woods ring again with mellifluous birdsong. An old woman crossed his path, burdened by a big pile of straw upon her back.

Tilman greeted her with a slight bow and saw a fleeting image of a long-lost young girl in her old, withered face. He had a flash of supernatural understanding about this old woman. Tilman realized it was better not to disturb somebody who had given up all her dreams for a simple existence without hope and destiny. He saw clearly the once beautiful woman still shimmering through the wrinkled face, a girl who dreamt many years before of different pastures and a life with a man who would give her love and children. But she buried it over decades of despair, hardened with the daily struggle to find food, wash, cook, and clean the modest house her parents left her when they died in the black death. No man or child ever entered her life. She blessed Tilman while the sun disappeared behind a horizon tinged with a light orange glow and said, "People are afraid of turmoil. But you need to set fire unto your life and seek those that fan your flames. Do not let other people tell you that your aims are just dreams. Just start the project when it comes from your heart. Everything will help you to fulfill your dream".

He continued his path, wondering about the old woman's words until he found a burnt-out ruin in the ever-increasing darkness where he could spend the night.

He awoke at the first tender light, packed his meager belongings in his knapsack, and continued to Nuremberg. His stomach ached, and his head was light because of the absence of any substantial meal for days. Along the way, he had begged peasants and villagers for some stale bread; sometimes, he was given a watery cabbage soup or thin porridge in friendly houses where the women always felt some pity with the beautiful boy whose face showed so much inner pain.

The lightness of spring had turned into the heavy warmth of summer. Tilman walked on, always watching for peril on the way, but nothing dangerous had impacted his lonely walks. One day, something miraculous happened on his path. He came upon a man sitting in front of a chapel, deep in prayer. The man smiled warmly at him and gestured for him to come closer.

Tilman felt a strong urge to follow the invitation. Something about this man drew him in, and he imagined a special light shimmering above his head.

The man wore fashionable traveling clothes, more suitable for a prince than a mere traveler on foot. He introduced himself as Hans and invited Tilman to a feast of culinary delights he had only heard of being served to kings and bishops. Hans spread a large blanket and placed a roasted chicken, potatoes, mushrooms, and corn out of his bags on the woolen table. And if that wasn't enough, he added grapes and cheese and even brought forward a bottle of wine.

While feasting, Hans spoke of episodes in Tilman's life that he had never told anyone. He spoke of Tilman's childhood dreams, aspirations, and hopes, assuring him that everything had happened as it was meant to be. Tilman felt a sense of relief and inner strength as Hans encouraged him to pursue his goals and let go of doubts and fears.

Hans said: "With dreams, God speaks to us. Sometimes, he talks directly to our Soul, and these revelations lead us to change our lives and find their real meaning. You want to escape the pain, but no matter how fast and far you run, it has already arrived. Realize that the cure for pain is the pain itself. You will carry the Universe inside you when you realize you are a Saint in the making and cease acting small."

Hans took a sip of wine and bit joyfully into a chicken leg he held while continuing to speak: "The simple things are the most difficult. The tasks you do without thought are the most important ones. The people you meet passing by will be the most influential for you. The secret lies in seeing the reality behind the veil. To find your destiny, you have to find the omens. You need to start reading the signs and not doubting that they were left for you specifically. Try to understand their language. Sometimes they appear as a riddle, but you know the answer when you go deep into your heart".

After speaking these words, Hans fell silent. He lay down on his thick woolen blanket and closed his eyes. Tilman did the same when night fell onto the land, still wondering about Hans's words. He reassured himself that all would be well on his travels if he remained true to his heart.

When Tilman awoke in the morning, Hans was gone. However, he had left the uneaten delicacies for Tilman to enjoy for breakfast. Tilman feasted on all the beautiful items that filled his belly and gave him confidence in the goodness of life and the meeting of angels disguised as ordinary travelers.

Tilman's heart was filled with thankfulness and clarity. Just by looking at the horizon and imagining his journey to meet Meister Balthasar, he felt immense joy. He knew that the Master would take him on as an apprentice, even if he had to beg and do all kinds of hard labor to prove his sincerity. Tilman understood that his calling was to give his dreams of the Madonna a form so beautiful that everybody could feel the world's adoration for her service.

As Tilman continued, he noticed a power he had not realized before. The power of his inner guardian was constantly warning him. He felt something pulling him left when he wanted to go right at a fork in the road. Later, he often heard that marauding soldiers were on the road he did not take or that there were dangers through robbers in the direction he had wanted to go.

Whenever he met a fellow traveler and walked with him for some miles, it was always a feast to hear stories from a foreign land the companion had traveled. The faces of fellow travelers were etched with lines of joy and sorrow, each one a storyteller of their own existence.

What miraculous tales he heard- the story of the lost princess and the one of Aladdin, who found an ordinary-looking lamp that fulfilled all his wishes.

But of all the stories he heard, the one of Pygmalion, the sculptor who created statues so beautiful that even the gods would weep, became his favorite. Some of the fellow travelers he met made him feel an immediate bondage. With those, he shared more than the familiar road or the tree to cover for shelter in a rainstorm. But none of them became the friend he had always wanted, the one he could think of in times of loneliness, a friend he could long for to share his life with, like a prayer.

Pain and Despair

People do not find their own destiny. They find a used one, a fate that has been confirmed by many other people. People believe in the lies they are told. They have given up the chance to escape the fool's wheel by living an unlivable life.

Nobody compared to Julius, who instantly became Tilman's dearest friend. They shared a deep connection, recognizing themselves in each other. Julius was a talented fiddler, and his impromptu melodies were a breath of fresh air, a welcome relief from the body's fatigue. They both met along the road when the jolly fellow suddenly appeared.

From the first notes that spilled from Julius's fiddle, Tilman was transported into a magic, joyful world where any monotony could not last, and boredom was forever banished. With his pleasing and unobtrusive nature, Julius became a friend, cherished instantly beyond measure. His songs were a balm, healing any self-inflected wounds of deep sorrow or weary memories.

The two friends walked the road to Nuremberg. Julius dreamed of a thankful audience and the pleasures of a well-situated burgher's life with a beautiful wife and, someday, a son. The dusty road became a flower field of shared laughter and stories, punctuated by the beauty of the trees and the clouds, pointed out by Julius, who always saw the hidden pleasures along the road.

They walked peacefully and merrily along their path when a troop of robbers suddenly appeared, brandishing their spears and knives. Julius and Tilman ran for their lives, and when Julius saw the murderers coming closer, he stopped in his run, shouting a breathless word of love to Tilman and begging him to continue to run. He threw his strong body into the oncoming pack of assassins, made them fall over their feet, and stopped their pursuit for some crucial minutes to give Tilman the advantage to get away.

This tragedy happened in the blink of an eye. Tilman's heart seemed to burst at the sudden realization of his cowardliness, devastated by the inevitable death of his beloved friend. He had been unable to stop his feet and turn back; the wish to live was too strong for him to conquer. He ran until he fell exhausted into a small trench, where he hid his body with leaves and twigs. The night came while his body was shivering and his heart throbbing with guilt and despair. He listened carefully to every noise, but none of the robbers came near his hide-out.

~

Tilman was alone; his world had collapsed. He experienced his own powerlessness in the moment of unbearable suffering. Whacked by pain, unable to move, and feverish with strong spells of cold shiver, his whole being faded away. Shame and fear made him weep deeply for his friend who had selflessly sacrificed himself. Only God's grace could save him now, but all his begging for forgiveness was only answered with bitterness and self-hate. It was clear to him that God and the Virgin had abandoned him, left him behind like an undeserving wretch. So he lay in his misery, and even the moon seemed to have hidden its shimmering light from this undeserving savage.

The following day, when the sun was already high on the firmament, he left his hiding place and walked on like a drunk, a shadow of his former self, a moving brute who only had disdain and anger for himself.

The whole day, he cried and lamented. He hit his face repeatedly to feel the pain in his body rather than in his heart. Late at night, he crashed exhausted on a meadow beside the road, not even bothering to take out his blanket.

Like a madman, Tilman picked up a rock, hitting his chest while murmuring these words: "My brain and heart are filled with hate and turmoil. Who am I? My throat is dry, filled with dust, and no tears can come amidst all this wasteland inside me. My body has broken down and pulled apart. I am dead inside under this burden of loss. God has deserted me. No more angelic voices in my head; where are the signs of his benevolence and guidance to me?"

He wept until a glimmer of light appeared before his inner eyes. He saw himself in a glistened light, sensing sparks of divinity starting to heal his broken heart. The loving grace of the Virgin was lifting him up, and he transcended his coarse mind in a prayer of infinite bliss. He understood he was not yet ready to receive the grace he longed for.

A vision appeared in him; he saw a brightness like rays of a burning sun, and a sound appeared in his ears singing the Gloria of the world. This brightness made him consider another light that could take all his sadness and anguish away.

Words of forgiveness and prayer formed on his lips: "I am twisting and writhing in my chain that holds me in its hard grip. Only my prayers and my love can weaken it. The trifles of my worthless life and the afflictions of my Soul are tearing my flesh apart. I long to become deaf to the vile whispers of my impure heart. Only the grace of God can free me from this burden."

In a flash, Tilman realized something shifting in his understanding of himself in this world. He needed to learn to have faith with modesty and repress audacity. He longed to leave this self-made prison by realizing his inner strength in following a higher purpose, understanding that his life would unfold not the way he wanted but only in the way that was meant for him.

He needed to accept everything coming his way, learn who he was, and not flee into oblivion. Destiny had given him a blow, and time was too precious for lamenting and despair. His trust in the guidance of God would lead him further on the path. These horrible yet soothing moments of recognition made him a true seeker. He let go of being the poor victim and understood that all this had happened to him to make him strong and humble. These thoughts gave him solace, and he finally fell asleep.

A night beneath the star-studded sky calmed Tilman's Soul further. When he awoke the following day, he wished to accept whatever God had provided him: "I cannot despair every time I dislike the fate God has given me. I need to accept his wisdom. I am faithful to go wherever he is leading me. I have no money in my pockets; all my clothes are mere rags, but I have the strength to lead me to my destiny."

After these events, life for Tilman appeared a little more apparent, and he became more empathetic to the people he met. As he walked through villages and sometimes helped a peasant carry his hay or pull a cart out of a ditch, he could sense how the man felt, if he was happy in his life or if his unfulfilled wishes were nagging him. His wandering in solitude had made him more aware of his emotions within the beauty of the landscape. He started to see things as they were and not as they appeared. A new understanding emerged. The people in the villages, the flowers along the way, and the wildlife as curious as himself gave him joy. A new longing appeared within Tilman like a silent melody that played within the depths of his Being, urging him forward.

He was learning many new things. Some of them he knew from his life at home, others he had never experienced before, and he rejoiced about the richness of this world. There were the fields of lavender, the lush dark woods, the words people spoke, their behavior, and their way of greeting each other.

Relaxed and unhurried, he continued his journey. He

could now better read the signs and knew by heart which way to go. The land had taught him the lessons of a lonely wanderer, and he drank them with the thirst of a devoted pupil.

Burning of a Witch

Who has the power to bring us back into the realm of divine servitude? No container can hold two kinds of liquid. If you like to hold divine joy you need to pour out the malice and despair

Nuremberg, the destination of his dreams, was now only a few days away. He had heard so much about this free Imperial City from the villagers he passed on his way. He envisioned the beauty of the Imperial Castle, whose silhouette he fantasized in all its beauty, overlooking the city. This was, after all, the most powerful and important city in the Holy Empire of the German Nation. He had heard of the many foreign tradesmen coming to this important marketplace, especially on the route from Italy. His step became lighter, and he started to rehearse the words he would tell Meister Balthasar to accept him as his apprentice.

Daydreaming and happy, Tilman approached a small

village at the edge of a large forest he had just passed. When he entered the hamlet, he sensed a disquieting hush over the little wood cottages, and an eerie feeling took hold of him. A winding path led him into the heart of the village, and he started to smell the scent of burning wood. A chilling event was unfolding before his eyes. The little village square was a scene of a terrifying witch burning that seemed to have started just now.

In the center of this macabre spectacle stood a woman, her eyes filled with horror masked by a veil of tears. The flickering flames painted her silhouette with a frightening glow as she was bound to the stake.

A crowd of villagers stood around the pyre, and two priests held up a large crucifix for protection, shouting for the woman to give up the evil forces and come back into the embrace of the church and the Savior.

Tilman could not stand this horrible spectacle; he just walked with eyes fixed on the ground at the square's edge to escape the scene as fast as possible. Almost at the end of the small village, he saw an old man sitting in front of his hut, smoking his long wooden pipe and inviting him with a kind gesture to sit beside him.

He was thankful for a moment of inner rest in the presence of another human being, bringing him away from the haunting images he had just witnessed. Without asking, the old man, called Wilhelm, began to tell the story of Gerda, the burning woman, and tears ran down his cheek.

Tilman learned from Wilhelm that Gerda, an old widow whose benevolence in the village was well known, was accused of witchcraft by some unknown people.

"Any evidence against her was not told," said the old villager, "she was given a monition to confess and return to the church. Then they took her to the torture chamber and hung her in the strappado for two hours. When she was brought out and asked to confess, she swore not to know anything of heresy. Then they brought her again to the torture chamber, and after one day, she admitted.

She said she had gone to the Sabbath and saw many men and women enjoying themselves and dancing backward. An attending neighbor persuaded her to do homage to the demon in the shape of a dark man called Robinet. Under his persuasion, she renounced God and the faith, kissed him on the foot, and promised him yearly tribute. He also gave her a long stick and a lot of ointment. Then she would anoint the stick with it, place it between her legs, and say: Go, in the name of the devil. At once, she was transported through the air to the Sabbath. The demon changed to the shape of a black dog, which they all kissed under the tail. And the men had intercourse with the women in a brutal manner. They ate the meat of infants, danced backward in circles, and were given powders of the bones and intestines of infants to work evil on men and beasts.

Wilhelm continued to tell of Gerda's ongoing torture until she gave the names of those who were on the Sabbath. "She gave the names of 11 others, and they are tortured now as well to give more names. Now, she burns at the stake, and fear and devastation reign in our little village".

The Abbey

A true spiritual life is the freedom from the ego. Seek nothing, want nothing but instead assign yourself to divinity. But spiritual pride may invade you. He who wants God needs to be humble, understanding his sins. When you are in God, you do not need God

When Tilman finally said farewell to the villager Wilhelm, his mind and heart were disturbed and sorrowful. He could not understand that such cruelty was done in the name of God.

He found a small but comfortable crevice between two large rocks a short distance from the village and spent a sleepless night, haunted by nightmares of devils disguised as priests.

Walking along the road to Nuremberg, he heard rumors

of war coming, which might mean his way was blocked. He thought it better to hide during the day in the woods and only travel by night. And so he did, but he was willing and did not worry about these new obstacles. So much had he already endured that it had lost its scary appearance.

Coming now very close to Nuremberg, he saw in the distance an impressive Abbey on top of a hill, and he felt deep in his heart that he needed to stop there and ask for a bed to spend the night. As customary in monasteries, travelers were welcome to stay and receive a meal and bed even when they could not reimburse the monks for their lodging.

As Tilman stood before the large oakwood gate of the abbey, he banged his fist on it. After a few minutes, the gate opened, revealing a short, round-shaped cloaked monk. The Benedictine introduced himself as Father Basel and welcomed Tilman with an open smile, beckoning him to step forward and enter the holy compound.

Father Basel was quite a merry man. He possessed a jolly countenance that radiated warmth and inner peace. The perpetual twinkle in his eyes hinted at a joy emanating from deep within.

Clothed in the simple brown robes of the Benedictine order, Father Basel moved with a surprising nimbleness that defied his large frame. His deep voice echoed melodically through the stone corridors. Tilman was fascinated with the enclosed courtyard surrounded by covered walkways, which serve as a space for meditation.

The outside world melted away for the tired traveler, leaving him with a serene embrace of contemplation by hearing a rhythmic murmur of prayers in the distance. Father Basel kindly offered to show Tilman the precious library with its treasures of scrolls and manuscripts. He mentioned that his monastery was exceptionally fortunate to hold religious texts and scriptures that go back to when the savior walked the earth. When the two entered the quiet, circular room, Tilman's nose was captured by the musty fragrance of the leather-bound volumes that held the enduring knowledge of centuries. His curiosity was sparked immediately, but he did not dare to touch any of the books for fear of breaking the untold code of restriction not to touch any of the treasures.

Father Basel told him the time had come for the monks to gather in the Refectory for their humble evening meal. As if to show Tilman the truth of these words, a bell rang in the distance, and slow-moving footsteps of monks could be heard in the near distance.

The Refectory was a simple stone wall, oval-shaped room adorned with faded frescoes of saints along its walls. A humble spread of crusty bread, root vegetables, and a plain broth were placed on the long wooden tables. The brothers ate silently, their faces reflecting a life of disciplined simplicity.

Amidst the quiet sounds of wooden spoons against wooden plates, one monk, seated at the head of the table, held a worn, oversized book. With a measured cadence, he read scripture passages aloud, the words resonating through the Refectory like a sacred melody. His voice added a layer of reverence to the communal gathering.

The Benedictines, their faces illuminated by the flickering light of a few candles, listened attentively as they ate. Their expressions, a blend of contemplation and gratitude, reflected the solemnity of the Moment. It was a shared ritual, a communion of both sustenance and spirit. As Tilman glanced around the room, he felt at ease with the harmonious scenery at this seemingly ordinary meal. He fell silent inside and finally found a place within him to let go of the horrible memories that had haunted him since he saw the woman burn at the stake.

After the meal, Father Basel led Tilman to a modest chamber. Its stone walls, adorned only by a wooden crucifix, had probably witnessed years of contemplation. A narrow cot covered with a coarse woolen blanket awaited Tilman for a night of rest.

A conversation spun between the two men out of nothing, giving Tilman a different insight into God's workings and a new understanding of his doubts and inner turmoil.

Father Basel felt that Tilman needed some words to ease a pain that devastated the boy. The monk began to ask his young guest, "You are on a journey to find yourself and your destiny in this world. What have you discovered so far about yourself?"

Tilman knew that he could talk to this brother without any fear. He began to tell the Father all that had happened to him since he had left his home in Eichenwald after his loved ones were brutally murdered.

Tilman wondered out loud: "How could my heart have betrayed me after so much suffering? What did those difficult months of wandering and witnessing such violence do to my Soul. I fell prey to the whispering of the ruthless snake who seeks to control me. I have given up hope for this brutal world and do not know anymore how to forgive and find my inner joy again. I see myself as a great failure; I am just a shattered clay vessel."

The Benedictine listened intently without interrupting Tilman in his flow of images and fears. After the young man had emptied his heart, Father Basel was silent for a few minutes, trying to find the right words for this seeker.

Finally, he offered: "The path of devotion is not easy, but it is in embracing its challenges that one finds true enlightenment. Doubt is always a companion on this sacred pilgrimage. Embrace it, for it is through questioning that you shall find a more profound understanding. Our faith is not stagnant; it evolves with every query and every challenge.

Refrain from disheartening if you cannot comprehend the lessons and tasks simultaneously. Allow the experiences to wash over you; with time, their meanings will reveal themselves like the petals of a blooming flower. The spiritual path is not linear. It twists and turns, and sometimes, it may seem lost. Trust in the guidance of God and seek solace in the silence of your reflections. In the darkest moments, the light of faith shines brightest."

These words soothed Tilman immensely. He knew that change comes to everybody, and God has no intention to break his children but only to bend them into the right shape. Father Basel prayed with Tilman to find solace in God and left the cell after warmly embracing the young man.

Tilman lay awake for a long time. A vision came, and he saw a brightness like the sun appearing in the morning glow. And in the same brightness, he saw another light that took away all sadness and anguish from him. He understood that Divine Grace could only be prayed for and must take root in the physical nature through his Soul.

A relief came over him, understanding that this vast and

inexhaustible world would hold the destiny of true love and heavenly bliss for him. With these thoughts calming his mind, he found the peace that allowed him to close his eyes and to find rest in the soothing glow of beautiful dreams of the Virgin Maria touching his old, withered face, smiling heavenly at him.

Arriving

I long for the open fields and the vast streams. Now the sun is setting on the rocks transforming into sparkling palaces in the evening laugh. I pray and long to arrive at my destiny

Tilman came to a long row of linden trees, like rooted clouds, pungent in the evening glow. He knew people usually dry the linden blossoms to guarantee a fragrant tea over the winter. But for him, they were his future saints or his beloved Madonna. Linden wood was his father's preferred material for carvings. Gunter had taught Tilman how to scrutinize every tree for its possible use and for signs of disease.

The day had had the warmth of the bright August sun, and suddenly, Tilman saw the Imperial Free City of Nuremberg in the distance. Standing like a stone behemoth, its spires and towers pierced the sky. The evening had come quickly, and the early rising full summer moon appeared with a glow in the early dawn. The linden trees shined with utmost vibrance like a heavenly halo. They seemed to Tilman like flowers of a good omen.

Seeing the city and his beloved linden trees together, he reminisces that this beauty has been denied to him for long: "My vision has grown now in its intensity of form and color like a burgeoning garden, seeing the city of my destiny in the distance. I have lost the ones I dearly loved, and the pain has changed the colors of my spirit. Their love has helped me become a friend to my heart; my destiny no longer frightens me. Now, I truly believe in you, dear God, and your urge to bring me spiritual perfection is answered in my Soul with jubilation."

With regained strength, Tilman walked on. He understood that a transformation had happened along the way, and he felt confident that his dreams would be fulfilled here and now.

He looked out at the horizon with tenderness. The mighty high walls of Nuremberg appeared now more apparent in the distance. The moon stood behind them. Nuremberg seemed awe-inspiring and daunting from a distance, a fortress of power etched in stone.

As Tilman walked through the city gate, he was thrust into a bustling symphony of life. The narrow streets were alive with the clatter of hooves and the calls of merchants. The air felt thick and foul, a scent of excrement combined with a mélange of spices, freshly tanned leather, and the earthy aroma of hay from the nearby stables. Torch-illuminated stalls lined the cobbled streets, displaying a kaleidoscope of goods. Merchants haggled with customers. Blacksmiths with soot-streaked aprons hammered away at their anvils. And then, amidst the activity of the tradesmen, some street performers captivated a crowd.

Tilman was overwhelmed after being on the road for weeks, experiencing loneliness only sometimes interrupted by a fleeting human encounter.

He sneaked into one of the stables and sought refuge for the night. The straw-covered floor offered a makeshift bed that cradled him in the darkness.

The following day, Tilman went to a little church nearby, hidden in a dark street corner with a large crucifix announcing its identity. Tilman went in and asked for the workshop of the famous sculptor Meister Balthasar. The frail, old priest sent him in the right direction, and Tilman, now heavy with the burden of insecurity and fear, arrived at an expensive-looking building whose ownership was announced by a large wooden plate: "Meister Balthasar - Artist and Sculptor."

Entering the workshop, Tilman found a young boy of maybe thirteen years sitting near the entrance and asked him where to find the Master. He was directed with an outstretched hand to a tall, muscular man standing at a long wooden table. There was a moment of silence and recognition in Tilman when he saw Meister Balthasar. It was so profound and piercing that he knew that destiny was speaking.

Tall and broad-shouldered, the woodcutter easily carried the weight of his fifty years, an athletic frame weathered by years of sculpting and crafting. His large, rough hands were most predominant. Sharp cheekbones framed a square jaw, conveying a sense of authority softened only by the warmth in his eyes.

His piercing gaze, a blend of intensity and contemplation, hinted at a mind constantly seeking perfection in artistic vision. Balthasar's salt-and-pepper hair fell in unruly waves. The dust of wood and the scent of resin clung to his simple clothes.

Approaching the master sculptor, Tilman cleared his throat. "Meister Balthasar," he began, his voice steady, "I seek to become your apprentice. I envision crafting the most beautiful Madonna the world has ever seen."

Balthasar, unmoved, continued to shape a piece of wood with practiced precision. "Visions are common among dreamers. What sets yours apart?"

Tilman, undeterred, spoke of his love for the craft, his years of honing the skills passed down by his father, and the burning desire to elevate his artistry under Balthasar's guidance. He painted a vivid picture of the Madonna, a sculpture that would transcend the mundane and reflect the divine.

Though initially indifferent, Balthasar couldn't deny the earnestness in Tilman's plea. He paused, studying the fire in the young man's eyes. "Crafting the most beautiful Madonna is no small feat. It requires dedication and skill. The divine is not easily conquered. Why should I take you on?"

With unwavering conviction, Tilman spoke of his journey, sacrifices, and visions that had become a beacon in his darkest moments. He shared the pain of losing his friend to the hands of robbers and the epiphany that followed – a revelation that art was not merely a pursuit of beauty but a journey of acceptance and resilience.

Balthasar, finally intrigued, regarded Tilman with a

newfound interest. At this moment, their gazes met, a connection was forged, and time held its breath. "A beautiful Madonna, crafted with conviction and deep inner love, will transcend the physical realm. Very well. Prove your dedication, and you shall be my apprentice."

The Work

You can have an empire of dirt or a kingdom of presence.
Understand the meaning of your life, accept the pain and break
time and death with your awakening

M eister Balthasar awoke early, as it was his custom,
with the same anxiety that had haunted him for the
last few years. His hands, once steady, betrayed a subtle tremor
as he traced the contours of a Madonna, standing beside his
bed, that bore a striking resemblance to his late wife,
Gertrude. She had been the pillar and soul of his life and was
taken from him. His son, the beloved little Kunert, who
should have been his successor, was also gone, thrown in a
mass grave.

Since they were both taken by the plague, the ache of loss,
now a constant companion, gripped his heart. He lived only
for his sculptures now. The house, once echoing with the

41

laughter of a merry family, had become quiet. Only his sculptures adorned the dark walls, reflecting the bittersweet symphony of memories etched in his heart. He had last sold one of his creations one year ago. He could not let them go, hanging on to them as anchors to a joyful past.

The arrival of Tilman heralded the prospect of a new chapter in his life. He had sent all his apprentices away, wanting to be alone in his pain. But this boy was different. His earnest wish to learn the trade, his love for the beauty of life, and his kind and lovely being rejuvenated the sculptor. He felt that a new beginning was possible. Spring had come into his heart. "Maybe this boy could be the one who will be able to follow in my footsteps," he thought. Tilman reminded him of himself when he was full of anticipation and dreams at the beginning of his quest. "It is never too late to change," he said to himself and decided to let Tilman finally become the apprentice he wanted to show all the skills he had learned on his long woodcutting journey. These thoughts gave him peace and joy, and he smiled for the first time in a year.

Tilman – like his Master - awoke before dawn regularly. It had been three months since he started his apprenticeship with Meister Balthasar. But this was not the training he had imagined. He was given a little room in the vast house and was commissioned to make the fire in the morning, clean the workshop, and feed the cow, the two sheep, and the five chickens in the adjacent stables. No real woodcutting task had been appointed, but Tilman knew in his heart that this time was a period proving his dedication by fulfilling all the low work with the utmost excellence.

On this particular morning, he sat silently for some time; the house was still sleeping. He thought of nothing in particular; he just let the cool air of a November morning wrap around him. The sound of the wind brought the scent of winter, and he understood that something would reveal itself to him.

When he met Meister Balthasar for a simple breakfast of oats and bread, he sensed a change in the air. His premonition was confirmed when the sculptor told him that today was the beginning of his apprenticeship.

As Tilman stepped into the workshop, a sanctuary for Master and apprentice, the air crackled with the anticipation of discovery. The seasoned scent of aged wood mingled with the lingering fragrance of long-dried finishes, creating an olfactory symphony that danced around Tilman's senses. He inhaled deeply, his eyes alight with the joy of revelation, as if each scent unveiled a secret world within.

Meister Balthasar talked to Tilman for the first time about the "meticulous process of tradition and innovation, of the alchemy of skill and intuition that defined a masterpiece from the ordinary."

The lessons continued over months with the studies of the intimate language of wood. The unique qualities of each type, grain direction's significance, and moisture's impact on the carving process. Balthasar spent days introducing Tilman to the tools, the chisels, gouges, mallets, and rasps, each with a specific role. Always maintaining sharp edges and cleanliness as needed for precision was paramount. In addition, he instructed Tilman in the art of sketching and planning to transfer the vision of the mind into wood. In the first months, Tilman's achievements were simple relief cutting, where figures emerged from a flat surface and took on a three-dimensional form. So much he learned. He needed to immerse himself in symbols and iconography to reflect his work's spiritual resonance.

But the beginning was not easy. Tilman grappled with the obstinate nature of ornate carving. The wood resisted his efforts, mocking his aspirations with each reluctant chip. Frustration swelled inside him. But slowly, the shaping of forms became easier; he discovered the alchemy of emotion and resistance, the dialogue between nature and art.

The intricacies of different woods were slowly revealed to him: the need to concentrate and focus on the task without inner distraction, the love in giving tenderness to every stroke of the mallet, and the firm grip on the chisel without rigidity.

Tilman loved the perfume of the different smells in the workshop ardently. He bathed in the sweet aroma of freshly cut wood, showered in the earthiness of sawdust, and immersed himself in the subtle fragrance of wood finishes. His sanctuary began to unfold. He had never felt so happy in his life. Woodcutting was first an aromatic embrace and then more and more a dance with St. Claude, the patron saint of sculptors.

He never stopped dreaming about creating the most beautiful Madonna anybody had ever seen. The Virgin Mary still visited him in his dreams, and he felt that in her smile was a hint of acceptance for the life he had taken.

Tilman was full of enthusiasm and purpose with which he would accomplish this aim. He knew it had been his calling, believed and desired it all his life. He was more confident now; he felt he could conquer the world and awaken people with the beauty of devotion and belief.

He was closer to his aim, and time did not matter anymore. He was on his path and would never stop. "We never can know how long a part of the way will take," he thought, "I always wanted things fast, not realizing that everything takes its own time."

Devotion

*Beauty is the harvest of presence. Do not evade destiny, as
ordinary people try to do, but fulfill your true potential.
Remember when you were a child, uttering simple prayers. At
that time epic dramas were unfolding within you*

The chisel in Tilman's hand became an extension of his
soul as he breathed life into rough-hewn wood. Tilman
understood that a masterwork can only be achieved after years
of learning, trying, and experimenting. His youthful approach
had been only the excitement of a boy. Now, he had become a
man, an artist in the making. Working diligently on different
assignments, Tilman connected his work with a more
significant calling in his life. He understood that one must
first give up the vanities in the world to purify oneself from
sins. This purification could only be learned through daily
devotion to hard work, kindness, and inner stillness. He

created daily aims for his salvation: to forgive others, to share one's bread, to commit no crime, to be kind, and above all, to believe in the mercy of God.

Tilman was constantly tested for his persistence and dedication to the trade. He had to patiently follow the tasks given to him meticulously by his Master and see the signs of real art appearing amid trials and errors. Often, Meister Balthasar spoke to him during their evening meal after the day's work was done and stillness had entered the house. But this stillness was now filled with a new joy. Life had returned to it, and Balthasar knew too well that his new apprentice was the reason for this unique gift, a new beginning.

Often in the evenings, the two artists spoke of creating unique artworks called 'masterworks,' bringing people from far away to see them. "One has to be consistent, persistent, and willing to study the human body deeply," said the Master, "and connect to the divine consciousness that we need to create something that truly touches men." He added, "Whoever connects to the Godlike energy can understand everything in this world. The world speaks many languages. A tree can be a shade or a tool to hang a man. A man can be a friend or the one that kills you. People become fascinated with words and objects and forget the language of the world. Art comes from pure life, a life of dedication and worship. A true masterwork does not have any ambivalence. Everybody who sees it is touched with the same emotion, connected to the Holy Spirit."

~

Tilman knew from the chatters of neighbors that Meister Balthasar's workshop had been frequented by bishops, princes, and even a king when King Albert II had visited Nuremberg. All these men in high positions had come to the 'Church of Our Lady' to see the famous altarpiece of the 'Augustinians' that had carried the name of Meister Balthasar far beyond the city gates of the Imperial town.

Meister Balthasar thanked Tilman in his calm and deep voice, saying he had become involved again in life through him. "I am immersed in my present life. My happiness is now to be only concerned with what is now. And I thank you, dear Tilman, for teaching me this essential element in a man's life."

Feeling the joy of spending evenings with his young apprentice who had become his adopted son, he continued: "The future belongs to God, and only he can reveal it at special moments. Even seers are only guessing because the thick veil can only be lifted partially between now and then. Only when we focus on the present and try to improve what is in the moment can we influence the future? Live each day by the scriptures, and have the example of the Savior as your guide. Only then can each day unfold within God's love. When you become his instrument, the future, past, and presence are one."

The Burgrave

Power always corrupts. No man can escape this curse

T he Burgrave of Nuremberg was a powerful man. Frederick VI had been small and sickly since childhood. He had a weak chin and no hair on his head, but his position gave him an appearance of power that no external features could diminish. His family had commanded the Imperial Castle over the town for three generations. The Burg was the symbol of control and authority in Nuremberg; its imposing walls and towers represented the power of the Holy Roman Empire of the German Nation. Its luxurious interior provided a fitting setting for the court of the Burgrave Frederick. Nothing happened in Nuremberg without his consent.

Meister Balthasar had been summoned to the castle to make a life-size statue of Frederick's Father, who had died quietly in his sleep two years ago. The master sculptor brought Tilman, and the chamberlain led them into the audience hall. The hall in the castle's heart was an impressive room with high ceilings and richly decorated walls. The floors were covered with the most beautiful carpets. From the top of the ceiling hung massive candelabras with beautiful crystals that flickered in the hundreds of lamps of hand-wrought gold, each with a lighted candle inside. Tapestries, paintings, and the family coat of arms hung from the walls.

The Burgrave rested on his raised throne with richly embroidered silk cushions. Dressed in fine dark red velvet robes, Frederick addressed Meister Balthasar to come closer. In short, demanding words, Balthasar was told what was expected of him. He would be required to finish the statue within three months. Payment would only be rendered if he delivered a work of art that would surpass any previous statues made by the Master's hand. With a leisure wink, Frederick indicated the audience to be finished.

The chamberlain was used to these short and abrupt audiences and often tried to soothe the blows his Master was handing out, especially with Meister Balthasar, whose famous high altar of Saint Augustin had given him so often a sense of awe and admiration. He wanted to talk a little to explore the sculpture's heart.

When he let the two men towards the exit, he leisurely mentioned his feelings and experiences at looking at the famous 'Augustinian.'

"Dear Meister Balthasar, every time I look at your marvelous altarpiece, I am taken away to the heavenly realms of our Savior. Your St. Augustine transcends time. His teachings resonate with me, his pure, heartfelt yearning for the divine. The chamberlain, Ambrose by name, continued to quote his favorite words from the Christian theologian: "Those who thirst to be with Christ ardently and never cease to hope for the eternal gift will receive the word. Hide me in your pavilion in times of trouble; give me your place of refuge as a shelter from storm and rain."

It was clear to the two artists that this man had experienced emotions of a higher order, and Meister Balthasar felt blessed that his art aroused these feelings in other men. He said: "Your words are balm to my own suffering. When one sees art as the true expression of God's divine guidance, it can lift us up to our dedication, giving the soul the peace it needs to ponder the meanings in this world." "Indeed," responded Ambrose, "St. Augustine delves into the depth of the human soul. His words carry a profound weight, and your carvings captured this spirit superbly."

Master and apprentice left the castle feeling honored. The castle's grandeur and the Burgrave's power had impressed them, but more so the chamberlain's words, who wished them farewell with another word from the Saint: "Our hearts are restless until they find rest in you, dear God."

Church of Our Lady

*Does not everything depend on our interpretation of the silence
around us*

Tilman had been Meister Balthasar's apprentice for three
years. After being instrumental in finishing the statue
of Frederick V, the Father of the current Burgrave, Tilman
was promoted in the sculptors' workshop and was widely
considered the inspiration for the master sculptor. After the
death of his wife and son, no work had been executed for
several years, but now his skills were again praised among the
people of Nuremberg.

Father Cristian, the priest of the famous 'Church of Our
Lady,' had considered replacing the Virgin Mary's humble
statue in the middle of the main altar with a new
representation of the Mother of Christ. He imagined a life-
size altarpiece, portraying her in heavenly beauty, holding the

little Savior in her lap and touching gently his cheek. The new Marien Statue should bring praise to his church from far and wide. He imagined the fame he would reap as the priest of this church, allowing him a little vanity besides his outward humility.

As he overheard some people talking about the new apprentice of Meister Balthasar and his aim to create the most beautiful Madonna ever conceived, he started to think. The coffer of his church was meager, and employing a Master like Balthasar, whose name and reputation first made him the premier choice for the execution, might drain the funds too much. But to hire the apprentice, whose first attempts were almost considered to be on even ground with the works of the older sculptor, made him silently jubilant.

Tilman still dreamed of the most beautiful Madonna the world had ever seen. His naivety and belief made him strong. His devotion allowed him to be foolish. But when destiny wants it, it appears in mysterious ways.

He had lived all his life for this. Every one of his days was dedicated to the love of his early childhood - the smile of the Virgin upon his face. He reflected on the different stages of this life. The marauding soldiers, the pest, Julius singing and playing his fiddle while wandering through the most beautiful enchanted landscapes.

Tillman had a vision that night when Father Cristian asked him to create the Virgin Mary for his church. A saint was visiting him in his dreams, speaking so frankly about Tilman's pride that he suddenly felt the cold wrath. "You must give up your selfishness and vanity to see the beauty of the Virgin."

When he awoke, he recalled the words and made drawings of executing his beloved Mother of God. "Now everything that is written must appear," he said silently. "I am just following my destiny. Even as a small boy, I knew I would create the most beautiful Madonna human eyes had ever seen. God tests all men. The challenge to stay pure and keep my faith is a constant struggle. By being humble, I will receive divine strength."

Falling in Love

*A candle has been lit inside of me for which the sun is a mere
trifle. The sweetest perfume has entered my Being*

~

This miracle happened simply, as all wonders usually
manifest. Tilman was wandering the market searching
for something to buy for supper. Then he saw her standing
behind her humble table laden with fruits and vegetables. He
approached her timidly, deep down, knowing that this
moment would change his life.

When Tilman saw Anna, the world stood still and came
forward, throwing flowers around him. He asked himself if
such a high love for a human vessel was possible. After laying
eyes on her, he immediately realized that the light of her
spiritual beauty blinded him, and he was stumbling towards
her like a fool to his destiny.

Tilman felt a scorching flame in his breast, a burning affection in his heart. This woman would belong to him; she was his inheritance of eternal love. The nobility of her conduct, her body's sweet beauty, and her kindness in her eyes made him faint. She would be his, wholly his, so he thought to himself. "She is full of colors. A lady so graceful and compassionate, complete with beauty and gentleness." He would worship her as a saint, so he swore, and this joyful madness filled his whole Being.

Finally, his earthly passion had been awakened; his spiritual love for the Virgin Mary belonged to a different realm. This miraculous woman would be his wife and the mother of his children. His faculty to love had been intensified by his gaze on her. His tender affection blossomed into love by the beauty of her smile. Her voice had made him deaf to any other sound; he only longed to hear her again and again.

Anna filled the market square with light and air. Her face shone like a brilliant star; a soft, clear light emanated around her. Her vibrant yet serene energy left a fresh perfume of youth and beauty behind her.

Tilman took refuge in a corner of her stand, not knowing what to do with his hands. Notwithstanding his nervousness, he could not stop staring at her. He noticed a delicious warmth creeping into his heart that expanded and erupted with every breath. He was uprooted like a tree in a violent thunderstorm; the gaze had penetrated his inner core and the soft, gentle smile on her rosy lips had shaken him deliriously.

He ran away; why? First, in small steps, one by one, in reverse. When he reached the end of the market square, his feet started to run until he got wet and exhausted reaching the workshop. But here again, he found her in his mind's eye, so beautiful, so good, and perfect. He was listening to the music of angels in an ideal world.

~

The next day, Tilman woke up confused after wet dreams had tormented him through the night. He needed to look into her eyes, see her body, and imagine the bliss of her touch.

When he arrived again at the market stand, sweating and out of breath, he started to utter the universal language of love. A force exerted itself when the two pairs of lovers' eyes met; a rainbow appeared without rain, sunshine followed, wrapping everything in its light, a moment of stillness shouted beyond the busy life, and all words ceased.

It required no explanation; the presence of the only woman for him took his breath. The recognition of a certainty that would never falter, a commitment that could never cease, wrapped him with fear and longing. Both recognized the same thing, and they smiled at each other without shyness, without holding back, opening the deepest realms of their souls to each other.

They had waited for each other all their life. The past or future became unimportant. They understood that God had written all this, and trust and confidence appeared in their hearts. Without such love, no dreams can have any meaning.

Tilman had loved her before he even knew that she existed. Her scent had been with him all these years, and he knew that with her, all the world's treasures would be revealed to him.

And then she started to talk to him. "What may I offer you, Sir?" timid words came out of her mouth. But for Tilman, her voice was more beautiful than the soft sound of the wind on a summer evening. He forgot everything about his past and only longed for the presence of this woman talking to him. He knew that he had dreamt since childhood about this wondrous present. Now it had arrived.

Her cheeks were rosy, her blue eyes were bright with the quick fire of life, and her delicate lips slightly opened. Oh, he loved her so much already. She was now part of his destiny and God's miraculous works.

They talked and gazed into each other's eyes, the timid talk of lovers who do not know each other yet but know everything anyway. They spoke of their dreams, their lives, and their favorite fruits.

Tilman just stood and gazed. He felt the rough stones of the square beneath his feet. Inside his body, a warm spring had filled his heart. He knew that everything was possible now with the love of this woman. He asked for her name, and she told him shyly that she was called Anna. Already, she had become the soul of the world for him. She had become part of everything for him; she was in his dreams, happiness, devotion, and most of all, part of his heart. This is the speed of genuine love when it happens.

The love he felt for Anna was distinct from possession. The concept of his love was more comprehensive than his wish to possess her. He looked up into the sky and saw a falcon rising above his head. A good omen his father used to tell him. Everything in this world has a meaning. "I need to learn the language of the world," he told himself, "and above all, I need to learn the language of love and what it does inside of me. It makes me finally the artist I had searched for so long outside of me."

Tillman understood what God was saying to him. He knew that at any given moment, God could reveal the being of all things to him.

Whatever he observed, a tree, a flower, a cloud, or his own hand, a connection was made to the world's meaning. "One needs to find a means of penetration into the unseen world," he thought, "and the world reveals itself."

For Anna, the affection she felt in her depth was imperceptibly stirred into a symphony of joy. She knew she was destined to love this boy who acted strangely at her market stand. She was full of him, and this was enough for her.

The Madonna

When Tilman started to imagine the most beautiful Virgin Mary to sculpt for the Church of Our Lady, it felt like a roaring wildfire in his soul. It crackled in his eyes and burned in his hardened hands, and he dreamt of shaping wood into divinity.

He thought to himself: "My passions are long and arduous. Where to begin is the most difficult, carrying the unknown within my feeble earlier attempts. Beginning this task frightens me. I ask for guidance but have not yet received any signs. Please hear my prayer and guide me to find the perfect lime wood. Lend me thy ear in this time of my deep distress. See how this life of mine passes away like smoke, how my rough hands are longing to form the beauty in praise of your grandeur. I am like grass that the sun has scorched. Come and rescue me."

He lay for days in his room, unable to rise and keep any of the food down that Meister Balthasar tried to administer to him. Nobody knew about his visions; nobody understood that God gave him this task. Nobody understood that he was expected to suffer, unaware of the bliss waiting for him.

And then he heard a voice inside him taking place. It says: "Just go into the forest, and I will guide you." He fell to his knees, and tears appeared in his eyes. He stood up, taking the heavy axe lightly, and just walked out. Angels were guiding his path.

Finding the perfect lime wood was all that mattered. It wasn't just wood; it was a living entity waiting to be awakened. He didn't merely search; he listened, his spirit attuned to the forest's energy. And then he found it, a majestic trunk, its knots echoing the call for his task.

His axe gladly vibrated when it met the wood. Each chip was a prayer to his muse within. Later, the workshop became his sacred space; the scent of sawdust became the incense of his dedication.

As Tilman worked, the wood seemed to respond, its fibers yielding to his touch, revealing the virgin's form beneath. He didn't force it; he just enabled the wood to appear.

Every chisel stroke was also a brushstroke on his inner canvas, every rasp of sandpaper a prayer for his beloved Madonna to appear. There were moments of doubt, of course. The wood might splinter, and the intricate form might elude his eyes. Every night, he stood before the unfinished sculpture, and slowly, the certainty of his masterpiece would grow inside him. He wasn't just carving wood; he gave form to a vision burning within him since his first inspirational spark.

And so, Tilman lived and breathed the Virgin Mary. He tasted her grace in the sawdust and smelled her purity in the gentle shavings. He was becoming one with his statue of Maria. His spirit became entwined with her human passion to reach the divine. The creation of his inner work reflected his calling. It became a gentle dance of creation between a man and his material to reach his ultimate prayer for grace. He talked to himself like a child, telling himself that his inner senses had opened to the sight of God:

"My eyes become alert to the beauty of this world. I am elevated by the rich silence of God's creation. He has revealed the inner workings of this world and my place in it. I know now that devotion and attention to the minuscule details are the path in understanding his quest."

Tilman had found his peace. In creating the Virgin Mary, he had carved a sense of belonging, a promise of the beauty that had revealed itself in his life. His inner joy had returned, and he hastened to embrace Anna and ask her to spend the rest of their lives together.

Epilogue - Pygmalion

~

Pygmalion, a gifted sculptor whose hands the gods had blessed, was known far and wide for his artistic creations that emanated breathtaking beauty and lifelike detail. But the sculptor, a man of great passion, yearned for something more profound than artistic admiration. He longed for a love touching his soul's depths.

His longing was unanswered, so he spent his days toiling away lonely in his humble workshop, forming stone blocks into statues of elegance and beauty. All who looked at his works of art admired them. Yet he felt a void within him, a longing for a connection beyond the boundaries of his sculpted masterpieces.

One fateful day, while wandering aimlessly through the winding streets, Pygmalion discovered a mysterious temple dedicated to Aphrodite, the goddess of love and beauty. As he stepped inside, his eyes were drawn to a radiant statue of the goddess herself, a masterpiece of marble that seemed to breathe an otherworldly aura. The sight of the figure stirred something deep within Pygmalion's heart. He was captivated by its ethereal beauty, its flawless form, and its divine presence.

At that moment, he was struck by the yearning to create a perfect sculpture so imbued with love and devotion that it would come to life and fill his world with the passion he craved. With newfound determination, Pygmalion returned to his workshop and set to work on his most ambitious sculpture. He poured his heart and soul into every stroke of his chisel, sculpting a figure so enchanting that it seemed to breathe with a life of its own.

The statue he created was that of a woman full of beauty and grace. He named her Galatea after the legendary sea nymph. Days turned into weeks, weeks into months, as Pygmalion poured his essence into the marble. His love for Galatea grew daily, and he whispered sweet words to her as he worked. Finally, the day came when Pygmalion completed his masterpiece. Galatea stood before him, a testament to his skill and unwavering love.

Nevertheless, a profound sadness wrapped him deeply. For he knew that his creation, no matter how perfect, was but stone, devoid of life and the ability to answer to his love. Devastated, Pygmalion fell to his knees before the statue, tears streaming down his face. He pleaded with the goddess Aphrodite, begging her to grant his deepest desire—to bring Galatea to life, to allow her to love him in return. The goddess of beauty and love heard his impassioned plea and was moved by Pygmalion's unwavering devotion. She looked down upon the sculptor and saw the purity of his love and the strength of his longing. And so, she begged her father Zeus, the Olympian Ruler, to grant Pygmalion's wish.

In a moment of divine intervention, the statue of Galatea began to stir. The stone slowly softened, giving way to supple flesh and warm breath. Galatea's eyes opened, and she gazed upon Pygmalion with love and adoration, just as he had always dreamed. Pygmalion's heart swelled with joy as he embraced his beloved Galatea. They pledged their eternal love to one another, grateful for the Gods' benevolence and the miracles they had bestowed upon them. Together, they embarked on a journey of love and companionship, their lives forever intertwined with this mystical and divine gift.

"*Your reality lies in the greatest enchantment you ever experienced.*"

Please Review

~

I am grateful that you read
"THE SCULPTOR".

**Did You enjoy Tilman's pilgrimage toward the presence
of God in himself?
Please do not hesitate to let other people know and
write a review!**

**Thank you,
Klaus**

About the Author

Who is Klaus Labuttis?

Experiencing his first Moments of Presence, Klaus felt himself come alive. A connection with a higher power appeared that has guided him through life since that moment.

Driven to discover his true self, Klaus has traveled and lived in various countries, including India, Central America, and Europe.

Over the years, Klaus has been involved in various entrepreneurial ventures across different industries and countries, such as Public Relations, Modern Classic

Furniture, Monarchs/Milkweed, and Health Travel.
However, his love for writing stems from his spiritual journey.
His first novel, "The Sculptor," reflects his transformative
journey of finding love and the meaning of life.

Currently, Klaus and his wife, Tanya, reside in Northern
California.

Contact:

MindfulKlaus@gmail.com

www.klauslabuttis.org

Discover my inspirational writings at https://
klauslabuttis.substack.com/

Also by Klaus Labuttis

SPIRITUAL CONSCIOUSNESS NOW

Bonus Book

***<u>The Sequence of Awakening - Ancient Conscious
Teachings Revealed</u>***
<u>Spiritual Exercises and Confirmation</u>

B ecause you have taken an essential step towards your Enlightenment by purchasing this book, I'd like to give you a little gift.

The Ancient Technique for Awakening used by Conscious Schools throughout history

The Sequence of Awakening

is the core of my daily practices to Be Present.
It is a powerful method to

Grasping The Moment
Giving Up Identifications
Experiencing My Life in Harmony With Higher Forces

In addition, I have added some exercises I use in different life situations that help me stay present and not lose my precious Self. It is designed for those situations where we are most mechanical, like eating, driving, or using technical devices.

Get it Now!

9 798988 873037